The Green
Magician Puzzle

The Green Magician Puzzle

by **Susan Pearson**

illustrated by
Gioia Fiammenghi

SIMON & SCHUSTER BOOKS FOR YOUNG READERS
PUBLISHED BY SIMON & SCHUSTER
New York • London • Toronto • Sydney • Tokyo • Singapore

SIMON & SCHUSTER BOOKS FOR YOUNG READERS

Simon & Schuster Building, Rockefeller Center, 1230 Avenue of the Americas, New York, New York 10020. Text copyright © 1991 by Susan Pearson. Illustrations copyright © 1991 by Gioia Fiammenghi. All rights reserved including the right of reproduction in whole or in part in any form. SIMON & SCHUSTER BOOKS FOR YOUNG READERS is a trademark of Simon & Schuster. Designed by Lucille Chomowicz   Manufactured in the United States of America
10 9 8 7 6 5 4 3 2 1   pbk. 10 9 8 7 6 5 4 3 2 1
Library of Congress Cataloging-in-Publication Data. Pearson, Susan. The green magician puzzle. Summary: Ernie and the other Martian club members hope to win the school contest by solving clues about the environment, which will allow them to appear as Green Magicians in the class play. [1. Environmental protection—Fiction. 2. Clubs—Fiction. 3. Contests—Fiction. 4. Schools—Fiction.] I. Fiammenghi, Gioia, ill. II. Title. PZ7.P323316Gr 1991 [E]—dc20 90-22436
ISBN 0-671-74054-7   ISBN 0-671-74053-9 (pbk.)

For Lorraine McIver,
a magician in her own right — SP

To My Family — GF

CONTENTS

CHAPTER 1

R.T. the Martian Smokestack

It was Saturday. Ernie was on her way to the Martian clubhouse. She was pulling her wagon behind her. Her dress-up box was in the wagon. Pollution was on her mind.

Room 123 was getting ready for Earth Day. The children were collecting cans to recycle. They were turning off lights to save electricity. They were picking up litter. Best of all, they were putting on a show. The show was called *Stop Pollution!*, and the Martians were going to be different kinds of pollution.

Ernie cut through Michael's side yard. The clubhouse was in the back. A sign on the door said:

MARTIAN CLUB
PRIVATE!
MARTIANS ONLY!
THIS MEANS
PRINCE MICHAEL
QUEEN ERNIE
KING WILLIAM
QUEEN R.T.
EVERYONE ELSE KEEP OUT!

Another sign said:

STAR FINDER
Travel Through Space
With Commander Michael

When it wasn't the clubhouse, the play-house was Michael's spaceship.

Ernie pushed open the door. Everyone was already there.

Michael was sitting on an orange crate. He was staring out the window. He was wearing an old set of headphones. That was how he talked to Mission Control. "Garbage in Galaxy Four!" he said. "Roger. We are on the way." He pushed some pretend buttons in front of him.

William looked up from his drawing. "Look!" he said. "I have drawn our costumes. This is R.T." He pointed to a smokestack. "You are air pollution, R.T. This is you, Ernie." He pointed to a garbage can. "You are people pollution. And this is me." He pointed to a raindrop. "I am acid rain."

"What about Michael?" said R.T. R.T.'s real name was Rachel, but everyone called her R.T. Even Ms. Finney.

Michael took off his headphones. He hung them around his neck. "My costume is a secret," he said. "It's really Martian!"

That Michael. He always had to be something from space. What was it this time?

Ernie wondered. Space garbage? "What are you going to be, Michael?" she asked.

"I told you," said Michael. "It's a secret."

"Let's get started," said William. "I brought the paper for R.T.'s smokestack."

He pulled out a giant piece of stiff white paper from the cupboard. He wrapped it around R.T. Then he drew circles where R.T.'s arms were. He drew a box where her eyes were.

"Now tape it together," said Michael.

"Not yet," said William. "We have to cut the holes first."

"And paint it," said R.T. "Smokestacks should not be white."

"We don't have enough paint for this!" said William.

"We don't need paint," said Ernie. "Follow me."

She picked up the paper. She marched out of the clubhouse. She went around to the back. The Martians followed behind her.

There was no grass behind the clubhouse, just dirt. Ernie spread the paper on the ground. She began to rub it with dirt.

"Neat-o!" said R.T.

"Mud will work better," said Michael. "I'll get the hose."

"Not too much water, Michael," said William. "You will make the paper all soggy."

Soon the paper was filthy. It looked great!

The Martians carried it back inside. They cut holes for R.T.'s arms. They cut another hole for her to see through. Then they wrapped it around her again. They taped it together.

"How do I look?" asked R.T.

"Just like a dirty old smokestack," said William.

"Except there is no smoke," said Michael. "You can't be a smokestack without smoke."

"Hmmm," said William. "You are right, Michael. Now what do we do?"

"Maybe I am just turned off," said R.T.

"That's no fun," said Michael. "You have to be polluting."

Suddenly Ernie had an idea. She dug around in the dress-up box. She pulled out a long gray scarf. She handed it to R.T.

"Pull your arm back inside," she said. "Then hold it up through the top."

R.T. did.

"Now wave the scarf," Ernie told her.

R.T. waved.

"Wow!" said William. "It looks like real smoke. We did it, Ernie!"

"I did it, too," said R.T. "I am the smoke-stack."

"Me too," said Michael. "I made the mud. Martian mud. Martians make the very best pollution!"

"So come on, Michael," said Ernie. "Tell us what kind of pollution you will be."

But Michael just zipped his lips shut. "It's still a surprise," he said.

CHAPTER 2

The Clue Contest

Ernie skipped to school on Monday morning. She had seven cans in her backpack. Seven cans to recycle. The can bin in front of school was getting fuller and fuller. Ernie's cans rattled with every skip. It was a good sound. A happy sound. A tambourine sound. Ernie skipped a little harder to make them rattle more.

"I am a walking tambourine," she sang. "A tambourine that keeps things clean.

I am a skipping tambourine.
I'm going to keep the planet green!"

She threw her cans into the bin. Then she skipped over to the jungle gym.

Michael was hanging by his knees. He did that every morning. That was how he practiced being weightless. His headphones were on, too. He must be talking to Mission Control.

Marcie was standing in the crow's nest. "I brought the most cans today," she called down. She tossed her head. Her yellow hair bounced. "Seventeen," she said. "How many did you bring, Ernie?"

"I'm not trying to beat anybody," said Ernie.

"I knew I brought more than you," said Marcie.

"Not more than we did, though," said Carmen. She and Geraldine were holding a big bag between them.

"There are twenty-five cans in here," said Geraldine. "We found them all at the park. There are a lot of litterbugs at the park."

"That doesn't count," said Marcie. "There are two of you."

Just then the bell rang. Ernie was glad. Who cared who brought the most cans, anyway?

The map was pulled down over one of the blackboards in Room 123. Ernie wondered what was behind it. A surprise?

"I bet you are all wondering what is behind the map," said Ms. Finney.

Everyone was.

"Well . . ." said Ms. Finney. "You all have parts in our show now. Four of you are Pollution." The Martians cheered. "Four of you are Litter." Jason's group cheered. "Four of you are Plants." Carmen and Geraldine and Marcie and Jo-Jo cheered. "Four of you are Land Animals." Sammy's group cheered.

"And four of you are Sea Animals." Ellen's group cheered.

"But there are still four parts missing," said Ms. Finney.

"You must have made a mistake, Ms. Finney," said Michael. "You have used up all the kids already."

"Right," said Ms. Finney. "So four of you will have two parts. One group will also get to be the Green Magicians." She picked up a green stick from her desk. It had a big green star at the end of it. "One group will hide these magic wands in their costumes. Then when all our plants have wilted and all our animals are sick, those four children will pull out their wands. They will chase the pollution and litter away. They will wave their wands over the plants and animals. Everything will be well again."

"Hooray!" shouted Michael and Jo-Jo and Carmen and Geraldine.

Ernie pictured herself in her garbage can

costume. She would throw off her lid. She would lift her wand in the air. She would clean up the planet. She would be a wonderful Green Magician. Maybe she would even make herself a magic green hat. She could make hats for all the Martian Green Magicians.

"Who gets to be the Green Magicians?" asked Marcie. "Why not make it the group that brings the most cans?"

Oh, no! Marcie and Carmen and Geraldine were all in the same group. They had already brought forty-two cans this morning. The Martians would never find more cans than they did. Ernie crossed her fingers. "Not cans," she whispered.

Ms. Finney smiled. "Not cans, Marcie," she said. "Clues!"

Clues! Ernie's tummy flip-flopped. She was very good at solving clues. Hadn't she proved there was no bogeyman in the old

yellow house? Hadn't she solved the lunch bag mystery? Clues were one of her very best things!

"We are going to have a contest," said Ms. Finney. "There will be four clues. The group that solves the most clues will be our Green Magicians." Ms. Finney reached for the map. "Your first clue is under the map," she said. "You have until Wednesday to solve it."

Ernie held her breath. Ms. Finney pulled up the map. There it was, Clue Number One.

> I eat dirt.
> I make the soil rich.
> There are 2,000,000 of me in the White Bear High School football field.
> There are ten of me in Room 123.
> What am I?

Ernie copied the clue into her notebook. *Hmmm.* She chewed on her pencil. The place to start was at the end. What were there ten of in Room 123? There were ten boys. There were ten girls. But boys and girls did not eat dirt. What else were there ten of?

Ernie looked around the room. There was one rabbit. Her name was Mrs. Lettuce. There were two hamsters. Their names were Fern and Flower. There were seven plants. There was one worm farm . . .

Just then Marcie turned around in her seat. The smell of Juicy Fruit gum blew into Ernie's face. Ernie held her breath again. She hated that smell! And she had to smell it every single day. Marcie sat right in front of her.

Marcie smiled her sweet, sticky smile. "The Plants are going to be the Green Magicians," she said. "Carmen is in our group. And Carmen is the smartest girl in Room 123." Then she bounced her yellow hair and turned around again.

"That doesn't mean the Plants will win,"

Ernie whispered. She chewed some more on her pencil. Carmen *was* smart, that was true. She was smart at spelling. She was smart at reading. She was smart at arithmetic, too. But Ernie was smart at something else. She was smart at solving clues. That was why they called her Eagle-Eye Ernie!

CHAPTER 3

The First Clue

When Ernie got home, Mommy was in the kitchen. "Hi!" Ernie shouted. Then she whizzed into her bedroom. She changed her clothes in a flash. Then she dashed back into the kitchen. She only stopped long enough to turn off the bathroom light.

"Where's the fire, lamb?" asked Mommy. She put a glass of milk and two cookies on the table.

Ernie stuffed a cookie into her mouth. She

took three fast swallows of milk. "Martian meeting," she mumbled. "Green Magic."

Mommy laughed. "Slow down, sugar."

Ernie took another swallow of milk. Then she told Mommy all about the Green Magicians and the clue contest and the ten things that ate dirt.

"And there are two million of them in the football field?" Mommy asked.

Ernie nodded. "Do you know what they are?"

"Not me!" said Mommy. "You are the detective in this house, Ernie."

Ernie grinned. "It was the ten in Room 123 that gave it away."

"What are they?" asked Mommy. "Aren't you going to tell me?"

"I have to tell the Martians first," said Ernie. "Go into the garden. Maybe you will figure it out there."

Mommy laughed. "You are a big tease, Ernie," she said.

Ernie hugged her. "I am going to be a Green Magician, too."

"You are my Green Magician already," said Mommy.

Ernie raced to the clubhouse. The Martians were sitting outside. They were digging in the dirt.

"I guess they are all at the football field," said Michael. "There are no dirt-eaters in my yard."

"Oh, yes, there are," said Ernie.

"You mean you know what they are?" asked Michael.

Ernie nodded.

"Tell us!" said William. "Then we can make my costume."

R.T. began to jump up and down. "I think I know, too!" she shouted. She whispered in Ernie's ear.

"We must be right!" said Ernie. "We both thought of the same thing!"

"What *is* it?" shouted William and Michael.

"Worms!" R.T. and Ernie shouted back.

"And there are ten of them in our worm farm at school, too," said Ernie. "I counted them last week. That was what gave it away."

"Hooray!" shouted Michael. "We have the first clue. We will be the Martian Green Magicians!"

"Maybe I will make us some magic green hats," said Ernie.

"First let's make my costume," said William.

The Martians went into the clubhouse. Ernie dug around in her dress-up box. She pulled out an old blue sheet.

"We can start with this," she said.

"Let's rub it with dirt, too," said Michael. "Acid rain should be dirty."

So they rubbed the sheet with mud. Then

they cut holes for William's head and arms. They made more cuts so the costume looked ragged and bad.

Then William tried it on. He twirled around. "How do I look?" he asked.

"You look bad, all right," said Michael. "But you don't look wet."

Ernie got out the colored markers. They drew raindrops all over the sheet.

"Still not wet enough," said Michael.

Ernie thought for a minute. What looked wet besides water? "I've got it!" she said. "William will carry a bucket of water. He will dip his hand into the bucket. He will sprinkle the acid rain all around."

"Let's do it now!" said William. "Then I can practice."

They filled a bucket with water. Then William danced around Michael's backyard. "I am acid rain," he sang. "Splash, splash, splash."

R.T. put on her smokestack. "I am a smokestack," she sang. "Smoke, smoke, smoke." She waved the gray scarf back and forth.

Ernie danced around the yard, too. "I will be a garbage can," she sang. "Pee-you, pee-you, pee-you!"

Michael danced, too. "And I will be a . . ." Suddenly he stopped. He clapped his hand over his mouth. "I almost gave it away," he said.

Now Ernie was more curious than ever.

CHAPTER 4

Too Many Green Magicians

On Wednesday the map was pulled down again. The children in Room 123 were hopping in their seats. Marcie was hopping more than anyone. She waved her hand in the air.

"Can my daddy come to our show?" she asked. "He is coming to Minnesota next week. From California." She wiggled in her seat. "*Please*, Ms. Finney?"

"I think that would be very nice, Marcie," said Ms. Finney.

Ernie was not so sure.

"But our show is in the afternoon, dear," said Ms. Finney. "Will he be able to come then?"

"He will come," said Marcie.

"We will send invitations to all the parents, then," said Ms. Finney.

Marcie waved her hand in the air again. Her yellow hair bounced. The smell of Juicy Fruit gum floated around her.

"The Plants have the answer, Ms. Finney," she said. "The answer to the clue."

"Marcie, put your gum in the wastebasket, please," said Ms. Finney.

"The Land Animals have the answer, too!" said Sammy. His glasses were slipping. He pushed them back up.

"So does the Litter!" said Jason. His feet were tapping under his desk.

"So do the Martians!" Michael shouted. "I mean, the Pollution."

"Michael, take off your headphones," said Ms. Finney.

"So do the Sea Animals," said Ellen.

"Will one person in each group please write down the answer," said Ms. Finney. "Marcie, you write for your group. William, you write for yours. Jason for yours. Sammy for yours. And Ellen for your group."

Five pencils scratched. Twenty children were silent.

Ms. Finney collected the answers. She read them. Then she went to the blackboard.

She wrote each group's name. Then she put a check next to Plants. Marcie and Carmen and Geraldine and Jo-Jo cheered. She put a check next to Land Animals. The Land Animals cheered. She put a check next to Sea Animals. The Sea Animals cheered. She put a check next to Litter. The Litter cheered.

Ernie held her breath. Would she put a check next to Pollution, too?

She did!

Ernie and Michael and William and R.T. cheered.

"Congratulations, everyone," said Ms. Finney. "You all knew the answer—worms!"

"Hooray!" everyone shouted.

"Are there really two million worms in the football field?" asked Jo-Jo.

"About that many," said Ms. Finney.

"Did you count them?" asked Michael.

Ms. Finney laughed. "No, Michael. I did not count them. I read it in a book."

"You had better make your clues harder, Ms. Finney," said Marcie. "There will be too many Green Magicians if you don't."

"Maybe this one will stump you," said Ms. Finney. "You have until Friday to figure it out."

She lifted the map.

When a tree is 15 years old,
it can make about 700 of me.

A big supermarket can use up
that many of me in 1 hour.
What am I?

This clue was harder, all right. Ernie had
no idea what it was.

CHAPTER 5

Brain Food

The Martians were walking home from school. It was a bright, sunny day. Birds were singing. Squirrels were chattering. Daffodils were dancing. But the Martians didn't care. They were too busy thinking.

Suddenly Michael jumped into the air. "I've got it!" he shouted.

"What is it?" the others asked. "Tell us!"

"Shhh," said Michael. "Come closer."

The Martians bent into a huddle in the middle of the sidewalk.

Michael took off his headphones. "Are you ready for this, Green Magicians?" he whispered.

Ernie and William and R.T. nodded.

"Toothpicks," Michael whispered.

"Yeah," whispered William. "Toothpicks are made from trees. And a store could use seven hundred toothpicks in an hour. All they would have to do is sell a couple of boxes."

But Ernie shook her head. "A tree makes a lot more than a couple boxes of toothpicks," she said.

Michael put his headphones back on. The Martians walked on.

Ernie scuffed her feet. R.T. chewed on her braid. William scratched his head. Michael listened to Mission Control.

Then R.T. stopped short. She spit out her braid. "Huddle!" she shouted.

They huddled again.

"What is it, R.T.?" asked Ernie.

"Fireplace logs," R.T. whispered. "Our supermarket has stacks and stacks of them. They must sell seven hundred logs in an hour."

"A tree could make seven hundred fireplace logs, I bet," whispered William.

This time Michael shook his head. "What about summer?" he asked. "Nobody buys fireplace logs in the summer."

Michael was right. The Martians walked on again. Soon they came to Ernie's house.

"Meet you at the clubhouse," said Ernie.

"I can't," said R.T. "I have to go to the dentist."

"Me neither," said William. "I have to get my hair cut."

"Me neither," said Michael. He groaned. "I have to clean my room."

Rats! thought Ernie. She waved good-bye. Then she trudged across her yard. She trudged in the back door. The porch light was on. She turned it off. Then she plopped her backpack down on the table. She plopped herself into a chair.

"Bad day?" asked Mommy.

"Hard clue," said Ernie.

"Cookies and milk?" asked Mommy.

Ernie shook her head. "I need brain food," she said. "Quick!"

Mommy handed her a banana. "What is the clue?" she asked. "Maybe I can help."

Ernie took a bite of banana. She did not feel any smarter. Some help would be nice. "But that would be cheating," she said.

"We won't cheat," said Mommy. "I promise."

Ernie told her the clue.

"Hmmm," said Mommy. "That is a hard one, all right. Maybe a trip to the supermarket would help. I have some shopping to do, anyway."

Ernie jumped to her feet. "Hooray!" she shouted. Then she remembered. She plopped back down again. "The Martians can't go today."

"Tomorrow, then," said Mommy. "You can call them up tonight. This afternoon you can help me in the garden."

Ernie unplopped herself. Banana brain food didn't always work right away. Sometimes it worked better the next day.

"I turned the porch light off, Mommy," said Ernie. "You forgot again."

Mommy hugged her. "I don't know what I would do without my Green Magician," she said. "Come on, now. Let's get out there with those dirt-eaters!"

CHAPTER 6

Fair and Square

On Thursday morning Ernie had five more cans in her backpack. She had two bananas, too. Her brain would be ready for the supermarket!

She hurried to the can bin. It was getting fuller and fuller. Ernie bet there were at least seven hundred cans in it. Too bad cans were not made from trees.

Ernie dumped her five cans into the bin. Then Jo-Jo dumped in four cans. Marcie was right behind him. She dumped in ten cans.

Carmen and Geraldine skipped over. They were holding hands and giggling. Had they figured out the clue? They dumped twelve cans into the bin.

"We are Green Magicians already!" said Geraldine.

Ernie's tummy flip-flopped. They *had* figured it out. She was sure of it.

"We have to win first," said Marcie. She looked at Ernie. "I think William cheated yesterday," she said. "I think I saw him look at my answer. I'm going to tell Ms. Finney."

Ernie's mouth dropped open. She felt her face get hot. What was the matter with Marcie, anyway? William did not cheat, and she knew it.

Ernie put her hands on her hips. She looked straight at Marcie. She stomped her foot. "William did not cheat!" she said. "We knew the answer was worms."

Marcie looked down at the ground. "I saw him," she said. "I am going to tell."

"You did not see him, Marcie," said Jo-Jo. "Ernie is right. William did not cheat. William never cheats."

"What were you doing looking at him, anyway?" asked Carmen. "You should keep your eyes on your own paper."

Just then the bell rang. Marcie ran off in a hurry. She stopped at the door and looked back at them. Ernie saw her wipe her nose. Was she crying?

Geraldine smiled at Ernie. "Marcie knows that William did not cheat," she said.

"She is just mad," said Jo-Jo. "Clue Number One was easy. But Clue Number Two is hard."

Ernie looked at him. Maybe the Plants had not figured it out yet, after all.

"Marcie really wants to be a Green Magician," said Carmen.

"So do I," said Ernie. "Don't you?"

"Sure," said Carmen. "But only if we win fair and square."

Mommy picked up the Martians after school. She drove them to the supermarket. "I have some shopping to do," she said. "You can walk through the aisles with me. Or you can watch the store from up front."

"Let's split up," said Ernie. "Then we will see everything."

Michael slapped her on the back. "Good thinking, Queen Ernie," he said.

Ernie grinned. Those bananas were doing their job.

Michael and R.T. went with Mrs. Jones. Ernie and William stayed up front.

"What should we look at?" asked William.

"The check-out counters," said Ernie. "Then we can see what people buy. You take this end, William. I'll watch that one."

Ernie walked to the other end of the store. She settled down to watch.

A lady came through with twenty-five cans of cat food. No wood there, just cans.

The check-out woman beeped on her cash register. The bag man slapped open a bag. He swished another bag into it. He rustled them together. Then he filled the double bag with cat food.

A man came through with five bottles of juice and ten cartons of milk. No wood there.

The cash register beeped some more. *Beep-beep-beep-beep-beep-beep*. The bag man filled three double bags this time. *Slap-swish-rustle, slap-swish-rustle, slap-swish-rustle.*

A lady came through with a pile of vegetables and fruit—oranges, apples, bananas, celery, lettuce, carrots, grapefruit. No wood there, either.

Beep-beep-beep-beep-beep-beep went the cash register. *Slap-swish-rustle, slap-swish-rustle, slap-swish-rustle* went the bags.

Tuna fish. Cereal. Mayonnaise. Soap powder. Cheese. Macaroni. *Beep-beep-beep-beep*. *Slap-swish-rustle, slap-swish-rustle.*

Spaghetti. Pears. Bread. Crackers. Cookies. *Beep-beep-beep-beep. Slap-swish-rustle, slap-swish-rustle.*

Ernie was getting dizzy. All she could hear anymore were beeps and bags. *Slap-swish-rustle, slap-swish-rustle.* What a lot of bags this store used!

Suddenly Ernie did not feel dizzy anymore. That was it. *Bags!* Paper was made from trees. Grocery bags were made from paper. And this store must use seven hundred bags in an hour. Ernie counted. They had just used twenty-two—and that was just at this checkout counter. Ernie looked at her watch. Only fifteen minutes had gone by. An hour was a lot longer than fifteen minutes.

Just then Mommy and R.T. and Michael came through the line.

"Find anything?" asked Mommy.

Ernie jumped up and down. "I figured it out!" she shouted.

"Shhh," said Michael.

"Huddle!" said R.T.

William ran over. The Martians huddled together.

"The answer is *paper bags*," Ernie whispered.

The Martians jumped into the air.

"We're going to be the Green Magicians!" they shouted.

CHAPTER 7

The Play

On Friday Ernie was early. Early enough to take the long cut. The long cut took her past two of her favorite places—the old bogeyman house and Twin Trees.

The bogeyman house belonged to Kate now. It didn't look like a bogeyman house anymore. Its shutters were straight. Its yard was tidy. It was painted yellow. In the morning it looked like a happy yellow sun on the corner.

Kate often sat on her porch in the morning. She was not there today, but Douglas was. Douglas was Kate's old orange cat.

Ernie waved. "I'm going to be a Green Magician, Douglas!" she called.

Next came Twin Trees. Twin Trees were two huge old pines. Their branches scraped the ground. Between them was a secret place. It was almost like a cave. Pine branches made green walls. Soft pine needles covered the ground. There were lots of pinecones there.

The pinecones were the reason Ernie was early today. She needed pinecones to make magic green hats. The hats would have leaves, too, and cloth flowers from her dress-up box. Ernie had them all planned out.

Ernie crawled under the branches. She took off her backpack. She filled it with pinecones. Then she crawled back out. She skipped the rest of the way to school. The bell was just ringing.

Ernie hurried to Room 123. The map was pulled down over the blackboard. She wished she could peek under it. She could hardly wait to see the next clue.

Ernie took her seat. Marcie was already in hers. She turned around right away. Ernie held her breath.

"Did you get this clue?" asked Marcie.

Ernie nodded.

Marcie sighed. "I thought so," she said. "What is your costume?"

"A garbage can," said Ernie.

"I am a flower," said Marcie. "I am going to be really beautiful." Then she turned back around.

Ernie breathed through her nose again.

Ms. Finney collected the answers after the Pledge. Not everyone had solved the clue this time. Only the Plants and the Pollution and the Litter had guessed that the answer was a paper bag.

Then Ms. Finney pulled up the map.

I have six holes.
I carry things in my holes.
When you throw me away,
be sure you cut me up!
If you don't, I might hurt animals.

Ernie almost jumped out of her seat. She knew the answer already. She was sure of it.

"Bring your answers on Monday," said Ms. Finney. "And now, push your desks back to the walls. It is time to practice our show."

The children pushed their desks back. Then they joined their groups.

The Plants and Animals were onstage first. Ms. Finney gave them all places. Then they acted like what they were.

Carmen and Geraldine and Marcie were flowers. Carmen and Geraldine swayed in the breeze. Marcie sort of danced around in the breeze.

Jo-Jo was a tree. He waved his branches.

"Tweet-tweet!" he called. "There is a bird on my branch," he whispered.

Sammy was a rabbit. He hopped around the room. He pretended to chew on a flower.

"Cut that out, Sammy!" said Marcie.

Tommy was a bear. "Grrrrr!" he growled. He held up his claws. "I am going to eat that rabbit."

"Try to be a gentle bear, Tommy," said Ms. Finney.

Ellen was a fish. She wiggled around on the floor.

"Now the Litter," said Ms. Finney.

The Litter ran onstage. They blew all around the room.

"And now the Pollution," said Ms. Finney.

Ernie and William and R.T. and Michael came onstage.

R.T. stood very stiff. She waved her arm above her head. "Smoke, smoke, smoke," she said.

William ran around the stage, raining. "Splash, splash, splash," he called. "Drip, drip, drip."

Ernie walked slowly around the stage. She held her nose. "Pee-you, pee-you, pee-you!"

Michael moved around the stage, too. He waved his arms in the air. He didn't say anything. He didn't look like anything, either.

Ms. Finney began to laugh. "Michael," she said. "Michael! Please take off your head-phones. Then tell me what you are!"

Michael slipped off his headphones. "I am a surprise," he whispered.

"I'll say," said Ms. Finney. "You can tell me during recess, okay?"

Michael nodded. Ernie wished he would tell the Martians, too.

It was time for the Plants and Animals to get sick. The flowers wilted. The animals looked sick. Sammy was a great sick rabbit.

He held his stomach. He doubled over. He made choking sounds. He looked wonderfully awful.

Ms. Finney was the Green Magician today. She came onstage. She waved her wand at the acid rain. William ran offstage. She waved her wand at the smokestack. R.T. ran offstage. She waved her wand at the Litter. The Litter ran to the garbage can. Then they all ran offstage together. Finally, Ms. Finney waved her wand at Michael. He ran offstage, too.

The sick animals got better. They danced around the room. The tree stood up straight again. It started tweeting. The flowers blew in the breeze.

"What fine actors you all are," said Ms. Finney. "You are wonderful already, and we still have a whole week to practice."

"We will be even more wonderful when we have on our costumes," said Marcie.

"We sure will," said Michael.

Ernie was more curious than ever now. What *was* Michael going to be? Maybe she could find out this weekend. But first, she needed to make a garbage can costume. And four magic green hats, too!

CHAPTER 8

Ernie The Garbage Can

The Martians met on the playground after school.

"Tell us, Ernie," said R.T. "What is the answer to the clue?"

"Shhh," said Ernie.

"You said you knew," said Michael.

"I do know," said Ernie. She looked over her shoulder. Marcie was sitting on the swings. "I can't tell you here. Someone has big ears."

"Let's go to Twin Trees," said William. "That is a safe place for a secret."

The Martians hurried down the sidewalk. They crawled under the trees.

"Now!" said Michael. "What is it?"

Ernie looked above her. There was no one up in the trees. She peeked out between the branches. There was no one walking by. "The coast is clear," she whispered. "The answer is, a plastic six-pack ring."

"A plastic six-pack ring?" said Michael. "Are you sure?"

"It has six holes," said R.T., "and it carries things."

"Can animals get hurt in one?" asked William.

Ernie nodded. "Yes, they can get caught in the rings. I saw it on TV. You should cut up the rings before you throw them away."

"Wow," said R.T.

"We know the answer!" shouted Michael. "We are going to be the Green Magicians."

"All we need is one more right answer," said R.T.

"And one garbage can costume," said Ernie.

"Meet at the clubhouse tomorrow," said William. "We will make your costume then."

Mommy was in the garden when Ernie got home. The back porch light was on again. Ernie turned it off. Then she came back to the garden. "We got the next clue," she said. "What are you doing?"

"Congratulations, sugar," said Mommy. "I am mixing this compost into the soil. To make it rich. It will make our vegetables grow better."

"Don't we have enough worms?" Ernie asked.

Mommy laughed. "I am giving our worms some help," she said.

The compost was in a garbage can. Mommy pulled the can to the other end of the garden. She left a trail of compost along the grass. "Oops," said Mommy. "There is a hole in my can. I will have to get a new one."

Ernie was starting to get an idea. "Won't you use this can anymore?" she asked.

"I don't see how I can," said Mommy. "Not with this hole."

Ernie's idea was getting bigger. "Can we cut it?" she asked. "Can we make the hole bigger?"

"The can is plastic," said Mommy. "I think we can cut it."

Ernie hopped up and down. Her idea was giant now! And she had not eaten a banana all day.

"Bong!" she shouted. "This can can be my costume. I will be a *real* garbage can!"

"Well, I'll be," said Mommy. "I think you have it. This can will make you a great costume. We'll clean it out. Then Daddy can cut it when he gets home."

After supper Ernie and Daddy went to the basement. Daddy cut off the bottom of the garbage can. He cut two holes for Ernie's arms. Then he cut another hole for her to see through.

Ernie stepped into the garbage can. Daddy put on the lid. Then Ernie paraded around the basement.

"My daughter, the garbage can," said Daddy.

"My daughter, the Green Magician," said Mommy.

They clapped and clapped. Ernie would have clapped, too, but her arms would not stretch around the can.

CHAPTER 9

Michael's Surprise

Ernie was up with the sun on Saturday morning. She had work to do. First she needed four hats.

"You can have my old fishing hat," said Daddy.

"And my old garden hat," said Mommy.

"How about a baseball cap?" asked Daddy.

"Good idea," said Mommy. "You can have mine, too."

Ernie found some safety pins and some

green ribbon and some glue. She grabbed a bag. Then she took everything to the backyard.

First she glued leaves all over the hats. Then she tied ribbons to the pinecones. She pinned them to the hats. They looked great. All these hats needed now were flowers.

The flowers were in her dress-up box. Her dress-up box was in the clubhouse.

Ernie put the hats in a bag. Then she climbed into her garbage can. Wait till the Martians saw her costume. Would they ever be surprised!

Ernie the Garbage Can walked to the Martian clubhouse. She pushed open the door. No one was there yet. Good. She could finish the hats before they came.

Ernie stepped out of her costume. She pinned two flowers to each hat. She put the hats back in the bag. She put the bag in the corner. Then she sat down to wait for the Martians.

Suddenly Ernie had an idea. Could she fool the Martians? She put on her costume again. Then she went outside. She walked to the side of the clubhouse. She pulled her arms inside the can. She crouched down so her feet would not show. Would anyone know it was Ernie? Or would they think she was a real garbage can?

Soon Michael came out his back door. He was wearing his headphones. He was carrying a box. He headed straight to the clubhouse. He did not pay any attention to Ernie. He just opened the door and went inside.

Ernie could hardly believe it. It worked. Michael thought she was a garbage can. What a great costume! Would she be able to fool R.T. and William, too?

Michael banged around inside the clubhouse. Ernie peeked through the window. What was he doing?

Michael cut the legs off some pantyhose. He stuffed the legs with old rags. Then he put gloves on the feet. He pinned them so they would stay on.

He was making arms! Were arms part of his costume? What kind of pollution had arms?

Just then Ernie heard William and R.T. Michael must have heard them, too. He put his things back in the box. He put the box inside the cupboard.

Ernie took her place again.

"Do you have an idea for Ernie's costume?" R.T. was asking.

"Not yet," said William. "A garbage can is hard to make."

They went into the clubhouse. They did not even notice Ernie. They thought she was a garbage can, too.

Ernie jumped up. "I fooled you!" she

shouted. She burst into the clubhouse. "You did not even see me out there." She pushed the lid off with her head. "You thought I was a real garbage can." She paraded around the clubhouse.

"Neat-o!" shouted R.T.

"That is the best costume I ever saw!" shouted William.

"The best costume so far," said Michael. "Wait till you see mine."

"Show us, then," said William.

"We want to see it," said R.T.

Michael shook his head. "Not yet," he said, "but soon."

"I have more costumes," Ernie told them. She got the bag from the corner. She pulled out the hats. "One magic green hat for each of us."

"These are great, Ernie," said William. He put on the fishing hat. "How do I look?"

"Neat," said R.T. She put on the garden hat.

Ernie and Michael put on the baseball caps.

"We will be the best Green Magicians that ever were!" shouted Michael. "Martian Green Magicians."

CHAPTER 10

The Last Clue

On Monday morning Ms. Finney collected the answers. Ernie was surprised. Four groups got it right. She guessed that a lot of kids had watched that TV show. Now the score looked like this.

Plants	✓	✓	✓
Land Animals	✓	O	✓
Sea Animals	✓	O	✓
Litter	✓	✓	O
Pollution	✓	✓	✓

The Plants and the Pollution were tied!

Ernie's tummy flip-flopped. She hoped she knew the answer to the next clue.

Ms. Finney pulled up the map. There it was.

I come from Africa.
You can use me to make soap
                and oil
                and ink
                and shoe polish
                and shaving cream
                and paper.
Or you can eat me!
I make good sandwiches.

Uh-oh, thought Ernie. This was the hardest clue yet!

At recess the Martians huddled behind the jungle gym. The Plants huddled by the swings. The Litter huddled by the door. The Land Animals huddled behind the slide. The

Sea Animals huddled in the field. All the groups were whispering.

"So what is it, Ernie?" whispered Michael.

"I don't know yet," said Ernie. "What comes from Africa?"

"Lions," whispered William.

"Nobody eats lion sandwiches," said R.T.

"Elephants?" whispered Michael. "Giraffes?"

"Come on, Michael," said R.T. "You don't eat elephant or giraffe sandwiches, either."

"Maybe it is not an animal," Ernie whispered. "Maybe it is a plant, like lettuce or something. Mommy puts lettuce on my sandwiches."

"My mom makes lots of tuna fish sandwiches," whispered William. "Maybe it is a tuna fish. Do tuna fish come from Africa?"

"They come from the ocean," said Ernie.

"I know that," said William. "The ocean could be next to Africa."

Suddenly there were four big shouts. Ernie looked up. The Plants were not huddled anymore. They were hopping around the swings.

"We did it!" Marcie shouted. "We know the answer. We are going to be the Green Magicians."

Ernie's tummy sank all the way down to her shoes.

The Martians met at the clubhouse after school. They did not find the answer. They walked to school together on Tuesday. They did not find the answer then, either. They were still trying to figure it out on their way home again.

"Zebras come from Africa," said Michael.

"Oh, Michael," said Ernie. "It has to be an animal that people eat."

"Like tuna fish," said William.

"What makes paper?" asked R.T.

"Trees!" answered Ernie and William and Michael.

"Then maybe it is some kind of tree," said R.T.

"People don't eat trees, either," said Michael.

Ernie stopped short. "They do if the trees make fruit," she said. "Maybe it is a banana. Do bananas come from Africa?"

"I don't know," said R.T. "But I don't think you can make shoe polish out of them."

"I still think it is tuna fish," said William. "You can make lots of things out of fish, can't you? You could use their bones and stuff."

"I think you can get oil from fish," said R.T. "I don't know about paper, though."

"You can get ink from squid," said Michael. "Maybe you can get ink from tuna fish, too."

"Maybe the answer *is* tuna fish," said Ernie. "We could try it, anyway."

On Wednesday morning Ernie crossed her fingers all the way to school. "Make it tuna fish," she kept whispering. "Make it tuna fish." Her fingers were still crossed when she took her seat.

Marcie came in right after her. She wiggled into her seat. Then she turned around. "Did you figure it out?" she whispered. She twisted a piece of her yellow hair around her finger.

Ernie shrugged her shoulders. "I don't know," she said.

Marcie twisted her hair harder. Ernie began to think she would pull it right out.

"Oh, I hope you didn't," Marcie whispered. "I hope, I hope, I hope." She turned back to the front.

She didn't have to say that, Ernie thought. It was a mean thing to say.

Ms. Finney collected the answers. She read them. Then she looked up and smiled.

"You have all done very well," she said. "I did not think you would solve any of my clues. And all of you have solved at least two. I am very proud of you."

"But who won, Ms. Finney?" asked Marcie. "Who will get to be the Green Magicians?"

"Only one group got the last answer right," said Ms. Finney. "That group will be our Green Magicians."

Ernie held her breath. She crossed her fingers tighter. "Please make it be tuna fish," she whispered.

"The answer is peanuts," said Ms. Finney.

"Peanuts?" said Michael.

"Peanuts!" shouted Jo-Jo and Carmen and Geraldine.

"My daddy will be so proud of me!" shouted Marcie.

"Can you really make all that stuff out of peanuts?" asked Jason.

"You sure can," said Ms. Finney. Then she told them all about peanuts and about a man named George Washington Carver. He was the person who found all those things to make out of peanuts. But Ernie didn't care about George Washington Carver. She was staring out the window. She was trying very hard not to cry.

CHAPTER 11

Magic Wands

"Let's go to my house," said Ernie after school.

"Okay with me," said Michael. He scuffed his feet along the sidewalk.

"Me too," said William. He kicked a stone. "I'm sorry."

"It's not your fault, William," said R.T. "Nobody ever thought of peanuts."

"Tuna fish was a good guess," said Ernie. "It could have been right."

The four friends trudged through Ernie's back door.

"Hello, Martians," said Mommy. "How about some brain food?"

"It is too late for brain food," said Ernie. She dropped her backpack on the counter.

"We lost," said R.T. She plopped down into a chair.

"I thought it was tuna fish," said William. "It wasn't."

Michael sat down on the floor. "It was peanuts," he said.

Ernie stomped her foot. "I wanted us to get it," she said. "I wanted to be a Green Magician!"

"Me too," said William.

"And me," said Michael.

"And me," said R.T. "I wanted to carry one of those wands."

Mommy sat down. "Come here, lamb," she said. She put one arm around Ernie. She put the other around William.

"You already are Green Magicians, you know," she said. "All of you."

"We are?" said Michael.

"Absolutely," said Mommy. "You have been recycling cans, haven't you?"

Michael and R.T. and William and Ernie nodded.

"And you have been turning off lights, haven't you?" asked Mommy.

"Yes," said R.T. "And now we are cutting up six-pack rings, too."

"To save the fish and the birds," said William.

"Well, all right, then," said Mommy. "That is what real Green Magicians are. They are people who care about the earth. They are people who save electricity. They are people who recycle cans. They are people who save animals. They are people like you."

"But we don't have magic green wands," said R.T.

"Real Green Magicians don't need magic wands," said Mommy. "You have been Green Magicians all along. And you never once had a magic wand. Your magic wands are inside of you."

Ernie thought about that. She liked it. A magic wand inside of her. It was green. And it had a giant green star at its tip. "Maybe we *are* Green Magicians," she said.

"You are the best kind of Green Magicians," said Mommy.

"We still have our magic green hats," said R.T.

"We still have the best Pollution costumes ever," said William.

"We are Martian Green Magicians!" said Michael.

CHAPTER 12

The Green Hats

"I can't find my smoke," R.T. wailed. Room 123 was backstage getting dressed.

"You dropped it," said Ernie. She picked the scarf off the floor. "Now push my lid on tight."

"I can't," said R.T. "I'm inside my smoke-stack, remember? My arms won't reach."

"Mine will," said William. He pounded on the lid.

"Not that tight!" yelled Ernie. "I'll never get out."

"Where are our magic green hats?" asked R.T.

"I almost forgot," said Ernie. "William, let me out of here."

William lifted the lid. Ernie climbed out of the garbage can. She ran to the corner. There were the hats, right where she had left them. She carried them back to the Martians.

"Here," she said. She handed R.T. a hat.

"It's beautiful," said R.T. She sighed. "But how am I going to get it on? It won't fit through my armhole."

"I can stand on a chair and drop it on your head," said William. "But no one will see it. They won't see your hat, either, Ernie. Not with your lid on."

"They will see yours, though," said Ernie.

William looked sad. "I don't think acid rain wears a hat," he said. "Not a magic green hat, anyway."

Ernie looked at her beautiful hats. She wanted people to see them. But William was right. These hats didn't go with acid rain. They really didn't go with pollution at all.

"Would somebody zip up my tree trunk?" said a voice. It was Jo-Jo. Ernie could only tell him by his voice. His head was hidden in his leaves.

Ernie zipped him up. Suddenly she had an idea. "Would you like to wear my magic green hat?" she asked.

Jo-Jo reached out a branch. He held the hat. "It is beautiful, Ernie," he said. "Would you really let me wear it?"

Ernie nodded.

"It can be a nest in my branches," said Jo-Jo. He stuck the hat among his leaves.

"It's a Magic Green Magician hat," said Ernie. "A Green Magician ought to wear it, and you are a Green Magician, Jo-Jo."

"The Green Magicians should wear our hats," said William. "Then everyone will see them."

"Good idea," said R.T. "Carmen! Geraldine! Marcie! Come over here!"

"Where's Michael?" asked William. "We need his hat, too."

"Here I am!" Michael popped out from behind the curtain. Ernie could hardly believe her eyes. She would never have guessed his costume. He wasn't pollution at all. Michael was a Martian!

He was dressed in green from *heads* to toe. Michael had *two* heads. Both of them were green, and both of them had flowers growing out of them. His arms were green, too. All *six* of them! They were made out of stockings, but they looked real. The stockings were painted green. The gloves on them were pink.

But best of all was Michael's sign. It looked like a giant green lollipop. In bright pink letters it said EVEN MARTIANS HATE POLLUTION!

Everyone said Room 123's play was the best part of the whole Earth Day show. It was in the afternoon, so not many parents came. But Ernie's mommy was there, and so was Marcie's daddy.

All the costumes were wonderful. Ernie thought she liked the Litter best. After the Pollution and the green-hatted Green Magicians, that is. The Litter were all covered with cans. The cans were tied together through their pop tops. They clattered with every step.

Carmen and Geraldine and Marcie were beautiful flowers. They were good Green Magicians, too. So was Jo-Jo. After all the plants and animals got sick, they put on their hats and whipped out their wands and made everyone well.

Jo-Jo was a terrific tree. He tweeted. Then he whistled from under his leaves. Jo-Jo's whistle always sounded more like wind, but today that was perfect. He sounded like the wind blowing through his branches.

Ellen's fish turned out to be a whale. It even had a blowhole.

Sammy the Sick Rabbit made everyone laugh, especially when one of his ears fell off. He didn't mind, though. Ernie thought maybe he did it on purpose.

R.T. the Smokestack and Ernie the Garbage Can received happy boos. Ernie hunched over inside her can. She tiptoed across the stage, just like a real villain.

William the Acid Rain got everyone wet, but mostly himself. Ms. Finney said he was the happiest acid rain she ever saw — and the wettest.

But Michael was everyone's favorite. The audience cheered when he came onstage. No one cared that he wasn't pollution. They liked him too much just the way he was.

When it was all over, Mommy and Marcie's daddy came backstage.

Mommy laughed and laughed at Michael's costume. "You take the cake, Michael," she said.

Michael jumped to make his arms bounce more. "The Martian cake," he said.

"Do I take the cake, too?" asked Marcie.

"You certainly do, Princess," said her daddy. He lifted her into the air. Her flower petals fluttered. Then he set her back down again. He reached behind him. He pulled out a bunch of flowers. He bowed to Marcie. "Flowers for my flower," he said.

"Oh, Daddy!" said Marcie. She grinned at everyone. "This is my daddy!"

"I understand Pollution was the runner-up," said Marcie's daddy.

"We didn't get the peanuts answer," said William.

"Can you keep a secret?" Marcie's daddy

asked. The Plants and the Martians nodded. "I would not have gotten any of the answers," he whispered. "I think you are all Green Magicians."

Mommy squeezed Ernie's hand. Ernie squeezed back. She felt like a Green Magician all the way down to her toes. A Green Magician hat-maker. A Green Magician Garbage Can. A Green Magician Eagle-Eye Ernie.